Funny Bone Readers

Cooperating

The Sunrise Band

by Jeff Dinardo

illustrated by Debbie Palen

RED CHAIR PRESS

Please visit our website at **www.redchairpress.com**.
Find a free catalog of all our high-quality products for young readers.

 For a free activity page for this story, go to
www.redchairpress.com and look for Free Activities.

The Sunrise Band: Cooperating

Publisher's Cataloging-In-Publication Data
(Prepared by The Donohue Group, Inc.)

Dinardo, Jeffrey.

The Sunrise Band : cooperating / by Jeff Dinardo ; illustrated by Debbie Palen.
  p. : col. ill. ; cm. -- (Funny bone readers)
Summary: Owl and Lizard are as different as night and day. Can they work out their
differences and band together? This illustrated story teaches young readers that working
together and cooperating can solve many problems. Book features: Big Words and Big
Questions.
Interest age level: 004-006.
ISBN: 978-1-939656-18-6 (lib. binding/hardcover)
ISBN: 978-1-939656-06-3 (pbk.)
ISBN: 978-1-939656-25-4 (ebook)
1. Cooperativeness--Juvenile fiction. 2. Musical groups--Juvenile fiction. 3. Owls--Juvenile
fiction. 4. Lizards--Juvenile fiction. 5. Cooperativeness--Fiction. 6. Musical groups--Fiction.
7. Owls--Fiction. 8. Lizards--Fiction. I. Palen, Debbie. II. Title.
PZ7.D6115 Su 2014

[E]   2013937170

This series first published by:
Red Chair Press LLC   PO Box 333   South Egremont, MA 01258-0333

Printed in the United States of America

1 2 3 4 5 18 17 16 15 14

Owl lived in the desert.
Her home was in the top of a tall cactus.

Owl loved to play the violin. She played at night under the light of the moon.

All the bats and foxes
came to listen when she played.

Lizard lived at the base of the same
cactus. He loved to play the saxophone
in the light of the bright sun.

All the prairie dogs and woodpeckers
came to listen when he played.

When Owl played her violin
at night, Lizard could not sleep.
The music kept him awake.

When Lizard played his saxophone
by day, Owl could not sleep.
The music kept her awake.

Lizard would plead with Owl at night.
"Please stop that noise!" he would yell.
"I need to sleep!"

Owl would shout to Lizard during the day. "Whooo is making that noise?" she would yell. "I need to rest!"

Owl and Lizard were both upset.
They both became too tired
to play their music.

Finally they decided to visit wise Coyote.
She was the smartest animal they knew.
Maybe she could help them.

Coyote listened as they each told their story. "There is only one answer," Coyote said. "Cooperate."

"How can we cooperate?" said Owl.
Lizard is awake during the day. I am
awake at night."

Just then the morning sun rose out of the
desert. The animal friends looked at it.
"I think I have an idea," said Lizard.

Lizard told Owl his idea.
"I think it may work," Owl said.
"We have to try!"

So every day before Owl went to bed she would fly down to the base of the cactus.

Lizard would be just waking up.

As night turned to day, Owl and Lizard
played their music together.

And everyone was there to listen
to the Sunrise Band.

Big Questions: Why do you think Owl and Lizard could not sleep? Coyote told Owl and Lizard to cooperate. What did they do then?

Big Words:

cooperate: act together toward the same goal

desert: dry land, usually covered in sand

plead: to ask with emotion; beg